THE INVISIBLE PRINCESS

FAITH RINGGOLD

CROWN PUBLISHERS, INC. ♛ NEW YORK

This African American tale of freedom
is dedicated to my three granddaughters:
Princess Faith, Princess Theodora,
and Princess Martha

Published by Crown Publishers, Inc., a Random House company,
201 East 50th Street, New York, New York 10022.

CROWN is a trademark of Crown Publishers, Inc.

www.randomhouse.com/kids

Printed in the United States of America

Library of Congress Cataloging–in–Publication Data

Faith Ringgold.

The Invisible Princess / by Faith Ringgold.

p.   cm.

Summary: Mama and Papa Love have a child, the Invisible Princess, who saves them and the other plantation slaves
from their cruel master so that they can all find happiness in the Invisible Village of Peace, Freedom, and Love.
[1. Slavery—Fiction. 2. Afro-Americans—Fiction.] I. Title.

PZ7.R4726In   1999

[E]—dc21   CIP

ISBN 0-517-80024-1 (trade)
ISBN 0-517-80025-X (lib. bdg.)

10 9 8 7 6 5 4 3 2 1

First Edition

Long ago, in the tiny Village of Visible, way down in the deep Deep South, there lived two slaves called Mama and Papa Love. They were called that because of the great love they had for children, though they had never had any of their own for fear that Captain Pepper, the mean old slave master, would sell their child and destroy their loving family.

One day, the Great Lady of Peace came to tell Mama Love that in spite of all her fears she was soon to have a baby girl, who would be so beautiful that she would be the envy of all who saw her. The Great Lady of Peace promised that this little girl would grow up to be a princess who would bring peace, freedom, and love to the slaves' Village of Visible. Mama Love was very happy, but she was frightened, too, for she knew that if Captain Pepper got wind of this, he would want to make the baby princess a slave. So Mama Love begged the Great Lady of Peace to hide her baby and protect her freedom.

And so the Great Lady of Peace asked the Prince of Night to conceal the beautiful princess in his great cloak of darkness and keep her forever safe from human eyes.

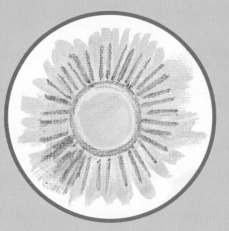

On the morning the baby was to be born, the sun shone brightly and the flowers blossomed and the birds sang sweetly and the bees swarmed and buzzed in chorus and everyone in the slaves' tiny Village of Visible could feel a strange sense of peace and love that they had never felt before.

As the beautiful baby princess came into the world, the Prince of Night appeared and spread his great black cloak across the sky, turning day into the blackest night. The sudden darkness woke the Terrible Storm King, who flew into a thunderous rage, releasing tumultuous rains and hurricane winds on the Village of Visible. It was during this storm that the Prince of Night wrenched the beautiful newborn baby from Mama Love's arms and disappeared with her tiny body into the stormy night.

From that day on, Mama Love, Papa Love, and all the slaves in the Village of Visible mourned the loss of the beautiful baby princess. They made a secret shrine in the cotton fields to her memory. They went there each day to remember the promise the Great Lady of Peace had made to them.

Captain Pepper's plantation was known as the richest and most beautiful plantation in the South. Although both white people and black people lived there, all the black people were slaves who worked from sunup till sundown for no pay, lived in broken-down shacks, wore rags, and had only discarded scraps of food from the slave master's table to eat.

On the other hand, all the white people wore splendidly tailored clothes, ate fine foods, and lived in beautiful houses. They sent their children to school while the slave children worked all day in the cotton fields and were forbidden to read or write.

One day Patience, Captain Pepper's blind daughter, was playing in the cotton fields and saw a little girl her own age. It made her so surprised and happy that she could see the girl that she ran home and told her father.

"Patience, my little blossom, you cannot see," said Captain Pepper.

"But, Father," said Patience, "I can see her."

"What does she look like?" asked Captain Pepper.

"She has nut-brown skin, shiny brown eyes, long black curls, and the most beautiful smile!" said Patience. "Everything around her glows. I know she must be a princess. Don't you believe me, Father?"

"No," growled the mean old slave master. "I have never seen a beautiful slave, and neither have you. You must promise me never to go to the cotton fields again."

"But why, Father?" asked Patience.

"Your mother was struck by lightning in those cotton fields during the Terrible Storm!" roared Captain Pepper.

"But why was Mother there?" asked Patience.

"She said she went to see a miracle," replied Captain Pepper.

"Mother went to see the beautiful princess who was born in the cotton fields, didn't she, Father?" asked Patience.

"No!" screamed the Captain. "Enough about this Invisible Princess!"

"Yes, Father," said Patience, thinking to herself: "That is just who she is—not a slave but an Invisible Princess."

Captain Pepper didn't want Patience to know it, but he had heard about the beautiful baby who had been born to Mama Love in the cotton fields, and now he was beginning to believe it. "But could there really be a beautiful slave, an Invisible Princess? Well, if there is, that slave is mine!" shouted Captain Pepper. "And I will find her."

Captain Pepper summoned his overseers to search the cotton fields, the slaves' shacks, and all the surrounding woods to find the Invisible Princess. But she was nowhere to be found. Captain Pepper was convinced that the slaves were hiding the princess from him. He vowed to punish them by selling Mama Love and Papa Love to different plantations so far apart that they would never see each other or their beautiful Invisible Princess again.

Hearing her father's vow, Patience went to warn the Invisible Princess that her parents were in danger. "I can see you," whispered Patience. "You are the beautiful princess who was born in the cotton fields. My mother came to see the miracle of your birth, but she was struck by lightning during the Terrible Storm and later died. Some people think you died, too. But I know you are alive because I can see you, even though I am blind. And now my father, Captain Pepper, knows, too, and he is trying to find you. He has threatened to sell Mama and Papa Love so that they will never see you or each other again."

The Invisible Princess realized she had to warn her parents. She found Mama and Papa Love praying at the shrine. "I have come here to help you," she began. "The Great Lady of Peace saved me just as you asked her to, Mama. But now you and Papa Love are in danger," she said. "Captain Pepper has threatened to sell you to plantations far away," she went on, tugging at her mama's apron.

"Oh, my beautiful daughter, we have prayed to see you again. Tell us what happened to you," pleaded Mama Love.

"On the day I was born, the Prince of Night hid me in his great black cloak of darkness, and during the Terrible Storm, he carried me away so that no one saw me leave. I was afraid, Mama, but the Prince of Night is very gentle and he quickly replaced my fears with restful sleep."

"Who is the Prince of Night?" asked Papa Love.

"He escaped from a slave ship by turning day into night. He is cold black and very handsome, Mama—and he is rich, too. His cloak is studded with diamonds that sparkle like stars. If Captain Pepper could see him, he would try to make him a slave. But no one can ever see the Prince of Night."

"You were just a newborn baby when we lost you. Where have you been?" asked Papa Love.

"The Great Powers of Nature take care of me, Papa. The Giant of the Trees made me a beautiful castle high up in his branches. And the Dream Queen visits me each night and brings me sweet, sweet dreams of freedom, Papa, dreams that one day will come true."

"The Sun Goddess wakes me each morning with fresh fruits and vegetables and keeps my days warm and beautiful. The Sea Queen brings me fresh water to drink and bathes me in mountain springs."

"The Great Lady of Peace teaches me to be loving, strong, and wise. And the Queen of Bees brings me fresh-baked honey cakes made with her special honey to keep me invisible."

"I am not afraid of Captain Pepper, because his power to destroy is no match against the creative powers of the Prince of Night, the Giant of the Trees, the Dream Queen, the Sun Goddess, the Sea Queen, the Great Lady of Peace, the Queen of Bees, and all the other wonderful Powers of Nature who have come to help us," said the Invisible Princess.

At that, the Great Powers of Nature made themselves heard. "Hear! Hear!" they chorused. "No one will harm any of you ever again. And from this day on, all of the slaves of the Village of Visible will be free!"

"But Captain Pepper is a very mean and powerful slave master. How can we ever be free of him?" asked Mama and Papa Love.

"I will make a batch of fresh-baked honey cakes with my special bittersweet honey," said the Queen of Bees. "Anyone who is stung by my bees and then eats my fresh-baked honey cakes will become invisible."

"And I will spread my great black cloak over the day and make it into the blackest night," said the Prince of Night. "And the slaves of the Village of Visible will disappear."

"Then the Invisible Village of Peace, Freedom, and Love will be born," said the Great Lady of Peace.

The next morning, in the slaves' Village of Visible, great bowls of fresh-baked honey cakes were left at the doors of all the slave shacks. A mighty army of bees led by the Queen herself swarmed through the cotton fields and stung the slaves, who then fled to their shacks and, seeing the bowls of fresh-baked honey cakes, ate their fill and became invisible.

Then Captain Pepper discovered that not only was no one working in the cotton fields or in the plantation houses, but also that Patience, his beloved daughter, was gone, too.

"Patience, Patience," roared Captain Pepper, "where are you? Come to me at once!"

But Patience had been in the cotton fields and had been stung and had eaten the fresh-baked honey cakes and was now in the Invisible Village of Peace, Freedom, and Love. There she could see the sun in the sky and the flowers in the fields and the trees in the forests and the people everywhere, and she was happier than she had ever been before.

Captain Pepper went every day to the deserted cotton fields in search of Patience. But all he could find were the bowls of stale honey cakes, with bees swarming everywhere. Captain Pepper could not hold back his tears as he cried out in grief for the loss of his only child, and in repentance for all the cruelty and pain he had brought to the lives of his slaves.

The Great Lady of Peace, hearing Captain Pepper's cries of remorse, came to his aid. "Patience, the Invisible Princess, and all your former slaves have a new life in the Invisible Village of Peace, Freedom, and Love, where everyone is free and lives in peace," said the Great Lady of Peace. "To be allowed to go there you must be stung by the bees and eat the fresh-baked honey cakes. Then you, too, will be carried to the Invisible Village of Peace, Freedom, and Love. There you will lose all desire to enslave and inflict misery on others. You have only a few minutes to decide."

"Oh, please, Great Lady, let the bees sting me!" cried Captain Pepper. "I'm ready to go and live in peace."

After Captain Pepper was stung by the bees, he gobbled up the fresh-baked honey cakes. And the Prince of Night appeared and spread his great black cloak, turning day into the darkest night. As a Terrible Storm circled the village, there were loud cracking sounds and the heavens split, and the Giant of the Trees bowed his head and lifted Captain Pepper up, up, up above the jet-black clouds of night into the Invisible Village of Peace, Freedom, and Love.

Patience was there with the Invisible Princess, Mama Love and Papa Love, and all the men, women, and children who had been slaves in the cotton fields and in the plantation houses and who were now free. There was music and dancing and storytelling, and everyone was happy for ever after.

Whenever you hear the buzzing of bees and you smell fresh-baked honey cakes and then suddenly day becomes darkest night and a Terrible Storm circles a village, you can be sure that an Invisible Village of Peace, Freedom, and Love has been born and that an Invisible Princess lives there. There are many such villages all over the world. And if you listen very carefully, you can hear the people of the villages singing:

We live
in a peaceful village
of freedom and love,
in harmony with
our brothers and sisters
by all the stars above.
We live in a beautiful village
full of happiness and joy,
dedicated to the freedom of
every man and woman
and every girl and boy.